Why Did Grandma Put Her Underwear in the Refrigerator?

An Explanation of Alzheimer's Disease for Children

Max Wallack and Carolyn Given

Fifty percent of this book's proceeds will support Alzheimer's research and the care of Alzheimer's patients.

Published by Puzzles To Remember, Inc.

ISBN-13: 978-1489501677
ISBN-10: 1489501673

Hi. I'm Julie, and I'm seven years old.

Here I am with my parents,

and this
is Grandma.

Grandma came to live with us when I was four. I was happy about that because Grandma and I always had great fun together. In fact, we were best friends. I have always loved doing things with Grandma.

I especially loved shopping with Grandma and coming home with cool new toys.

Back when I started kindergarten,

Grandma bought me a new backpack.

She took me to the bus stop.

"Have a good day in school," she said.

"I love you."

Every day after school, we played games together. On rainy days, we put together puzzles about happy, sunny days.

It was a cold, snowy winter that year, so we spent a lot of time in the house.

Sometimes I noticed that Grandma couldn't remember where she put things, and it made her very upset.

I thought that maybe it was my fault because I had so many toys around and my room was usually a mess.

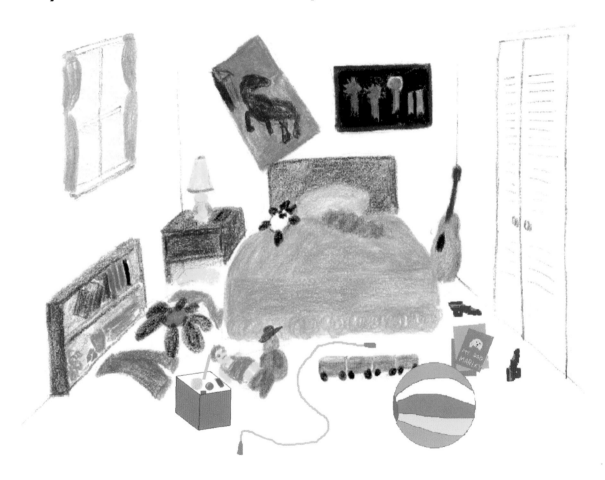

But Mom told me, "Grandma can't remember things because she has an illness called Alzheimer's disease."

Last summer, Grandma started putting things in funny places.

That summer, just before first grade, it was very sunny and hot. One morning, I woke up very thirsty.

When I went to the refrigerator, do you know what I found? A pair of pink underwear!

They were right there, between the milk carton and the juice. Grandma had draped them over the watermelon we had bought for our Fourth of July party.

I bet you think I was surprised,
but NOPE -- I've gotten used to
things being mixed up in my house.

I started worrying if I could catch Alzheimer's disease, but Mom sat me down and explained:

"No one can catch Alzheimer's disease from another person. It's just something that went wrong with the chemicals in Grandma's brain."

"The cells in Grandma's brain can't always throw and catch the messages the way they should."

Healthy brain cell

Brain cell with Alzheimer's disease

When the messages in her brain get through, Grandma seems absolutely fine. We still have lots of fun together. We went to the zoo four times last summer!

But when the messages in her brain get mixed up, things don't look the same to Grandma as they look to me.

Dad said, "It's like when you look at yourself in a fun house mirror. You're still the same, but the mirror makes

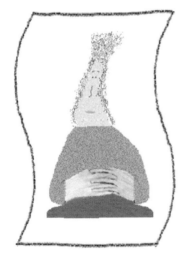

you look different."

One day, Grandma couldn't remember my name. I guess I looked different to her that day.

Let's go shopping today, Alice.

Grandma, I'm Julie. My name is Julie.

It only took a few seconds for Grandma's eyes to recognize me and smile. Then, she gave me a big hug.

Sometimes, Grandma asks the same question over and over again.

I know it's because she doesn't remember the answer, so I have to help her remember. I answer the question, and I tell her how much I love her.

Then I ask Grandma to go out with me for a walk. Walking outdoors always makes her feel better.

When we go out together, I stay very close to Grandma to keep her safe. She has been forgetting more and more things recently.

Sometimes, Grandma becomes frightened by silly little things. It's because they look different to her. Maybe the little kitten looks like a ferocious lion.

When this happens, I try to make Grandma feel better by telling her all about what I did at school. Pretty soon, she forgets about being afraid.

In October, everyone in first grade class was looking forward to Halloween. I was going to dress up as a witch for "trick or treat." I had a great costume all ready. When Grandma saw me dressed as a witch, she got terrified and started crying. I had to change my clothes, and I couldn't go out for "trick or treat" at all. I was really angry at Grandma.

The next day, I felt sorry.

I was angry at Grandma, and then I felt guilty because I know it's not her fault.

I'm sorry that I got angry at Grandma, but I'm also sad that my Halloween was spoiled.

One night in December, during school vacation, Grandma got up at night and went out all by herself without her coat.

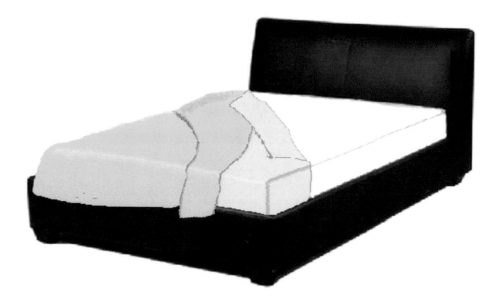

I was very worried when I learned that she wasn't home.

Mom said, "Grandma is probably having beautiful memories of her childhood, and she wanted to find the place where

she used to live so she could enjoy

more of those happy, wonderful times."

As soon as we found out that Grandma was missing, we called the police. They found Grandma and brought her home.

Now we have a bell on our door,

so we know if anyone goes in or out.

At the end of the school year, my
first grade class put on a play.

Grandma came with us. She was doing
very well that day and said she was
very proud of me. She was very nice to
my friends and told them about what it
was like when she was in school.

But the trip made her very tired, and she forgot to go to the bathroom. I was so embarrassed that Grandma wet the seat, and I had to explain it to my friends.

These days, Grandma is forgetting lots of things.

Sometimes, she forgets to eat. I got her a special red plate so that she can see her food better. I sit with her, cut up her meat, and tell her happy stories while she eats. She always likes that.

After dinner, we either do puzzles, or else we color and make drawings together.

Grandma never forgets how to make great drawings. I think she's an artist.

Grandma can't really stay home any more all by herself, so she goes to the Adult Memory Day Care Center a few days each week. I help her get on the Day Care Center's bus before I go to school in the morning.

I always wave good-bye and say, "I love you, Grandma; have a good day with your friends!"

At the Day Care Center, Grandma
has lots of friends who also have
Alzheimer's disease. They listen to
music, play games, and do art projects
and puzzles to help their memories.

This morning, my Mom said, "I am very proud of you because you are a very good caregiver." That means that, even though I'm still a kid, I'm being a big help taking care of Grandma.

I like being a caregiver because I love Grandma and I know she loves me.

I noticed that Grandma is taking pills every day.

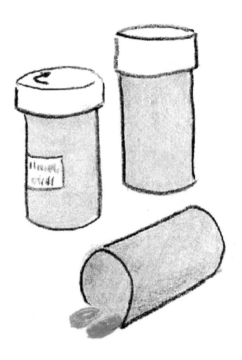

When I asked Dad about the pills, he said, "Smart scientists have found some medicines that can help Grandma. They can't make her all better right now, but they do help her feel better."

"And those smart scientists are working hard to find even better medicines."

"Maybe, in a few years, they might even be able to cure Alzheimer's disease completely!"

Maybe I will grow up to be one of those scientists, and I can find a cure for Alzheimer's disease.

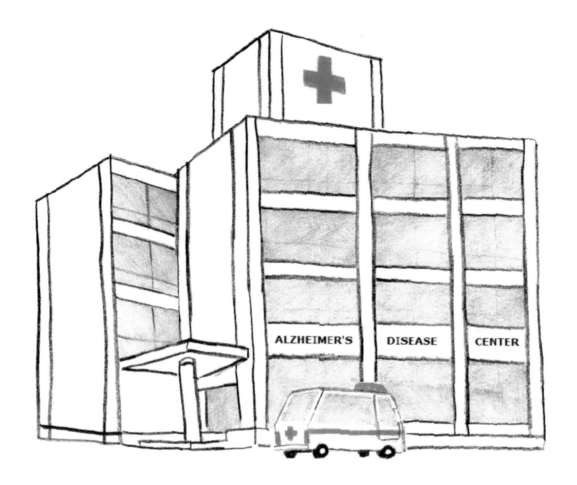

Starting soon, every month I will help

Mom take Grandma to a hospital where

she will be in a special research study.

That means doctors will give Grandma

new medicines to see if they can help

people with Alzheimer's disease.

If we can find a cure, then families won't need to worry about Alzheimer's disease any more.

Made in the USA
Lexington, KY
26 July 2013